DIRT BIKE WORLD

Freestyle
Motocross

by Thomas K. Adamson

Reading Consultant:
Barbara J. Fox
Reading Specialist
North Carolina State University

Blazers is published by Capstone Press,
151 Good Counsel Drive, P.O. Box 669, Mankato, Minnesota 56002.
www.capstonepub.com

Library of Congress Cataloging-in-Publication Data
Adamson, Thomas K., 1970–
Freestyle motocross / by Thomas K. Adamson.
    p. cm.—(Blazers. dirt bike world.)
Includes bibliographical references and index.
Summary: "Describes the motorsport of freestyle motocross, including tricks, competition rules,
and stars"—Provided by publisher.
ISBN 978-1-4296-5019-9 (library binding)
ISBN 978-1-4296-5630-6 (paperback)
1. Motocross—Juvenile literature. I. Title. II. Series.
GV1060.12.A37 2011
796.7'56—dc22   2010004167

Editorial Credits
Mandy Robbins, editor; Tracy Davies, designer; Laura Manthe, production specialist

**Capstone Press would like to thank Ken Glaser, Director of Special Projects for the Motorcycle
Safety Foundation in Irvine, California, for his expertise and assistance in making this book.**

Photo Credits
CORBIS/Bo Bridges, 25
Getty Images Inc./AFP/Alfredo Estrella, 10; AFP/Luis Acosta, 11, cover; AFP/Michal Cizek, 18;
    AFP/Tony Ashby, 16–17; Elsa, 15; Jeff Gross, 20; Jonathan Ferrey, 9; Quinn Rooney, 27;
    WireImage/Ben Liebenberg, 23
Newscom, 24; Icon SMI/STL/Jeff Crow, 26; Icon SMI/Tony Donaldson, 5, 6, 19; SIPA/
    Edgerider/C. Van Hanja, 7
Red Bull via Getty Images/Balazs Gardi, 13, Chris Tedesco, 28–29
Shutterstock/Margo Harrison, back cover

Artistic Effects
Shutterstock/Irmak Akcadogan, Konstanttin, Nitipong Ballapavanich, oriontrail

Table of Contents

chapter 1

A Big Win

The Best Trick event had begun at the 2008 X Games. Kyle Loza soared off the ramp. Loza is known for his daring freestyle **motocross** (FMX) tricks. Fans wondered what wild new trick he would try.

motocross—a type of dirt bike race held on outdoor courses

Fact: In 2009, Loza won his third gold medal in the X Games Best Trick category.

Loza's bike soared 35 feet (11 meters) into the air. Loza flipped backward, kicked his legs up, and spun around. Loza called his new trick Electric Doom. It earned him the gold medal.

Kyle Loza (center) at the 2009 X Games

chapter 2

FMX Basics

In the early 1990s, motocross racers liked to show off over jumps. Fans enjoyed watching the wild moves. The sport of FMX showcases these daring tricks.

FMX riders score points for doing tricks in midair. Judges award points for style, difficulty, and new tricks. The rider with the most points wins.

No-Handed Indian Air

Kiss of Death

Fact: Some riders add extra levers to their bikes. They grab the levers with their hands or feet during tricks.

Crashes are sure to happen in FMX. Protective gear helps riders stay safe. Riders wear helmets and knee guards. They also wear a chest protector and other body **armor.**

Fact: FMX riders practice new tricks over a foam pit to stay safe.

armor—hard covering that riders wear for protection in crashes

12

Tricks of the Trade

Riders invent new tricks every year.
Fans love the Cordova, Superman, and
Rock Solid. **Classic** tricks like the Dead
Body, Hart Attack, and Kiss of Death
excite crowds too.

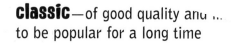

classic—of good quality and ...
to be popular for a long time

Fact: Chris Rourke invented the Rock Solid in 2001.

Fans love to see classic tricks. But only new tricks and **combinations** will score enough points to win. Combinations include the Catnac Indian Air, the Helicopter, and the Superman Indian Air.

combination—a mixture of two or more tricks

The backflip is the most difficult move. The best riders invent exciting backflip **variations**. These tricks include the Cordova Backflip and the Lazy Boy Backflip. Some daring riders even try the Double Backflip.

Cordova Backflip

variation—a slight change that makes an old trick a new one again

Fact: Travis Pastrana landed the first Double Backflip in competition during the 2006 X Games.

Instead of backflips, Kyle Loza does **body varials**. Loza won X Games gold with the Volt in 2007. He spun himself around as his bike sailed through the air.

Fact: Loza's 2007 win was exciting because it was his first year of professional racing.

body varial—a trick in which the rider removes himself from the bike and spins

chapter 4

FMX Stars

Travis Pastrana has been unbeatable
in FMX contests. He invented the Lazy
Boy, the Cliffhanger, and other tricks.
Pastrana has won six FMX gold medals
in the X Games.

Travis Pastrana performing the Lazy Boy

Fact: Pastrana won three gold medals in three different events at the 2006 X Games.

Brian Deegan performing a Seat Grab Indian Air

Brian Deegan is one of the sport's best riders. He was the first rider to try **sidesaddle** landings. Deegan has won three X Games FMX gold medals.

Brian Deegan at Winter X Games 2004

Fact: Deegan is best known for inventing the Mulisha Twist.

sidesaddle—when a rider has both feet on one side of the bike

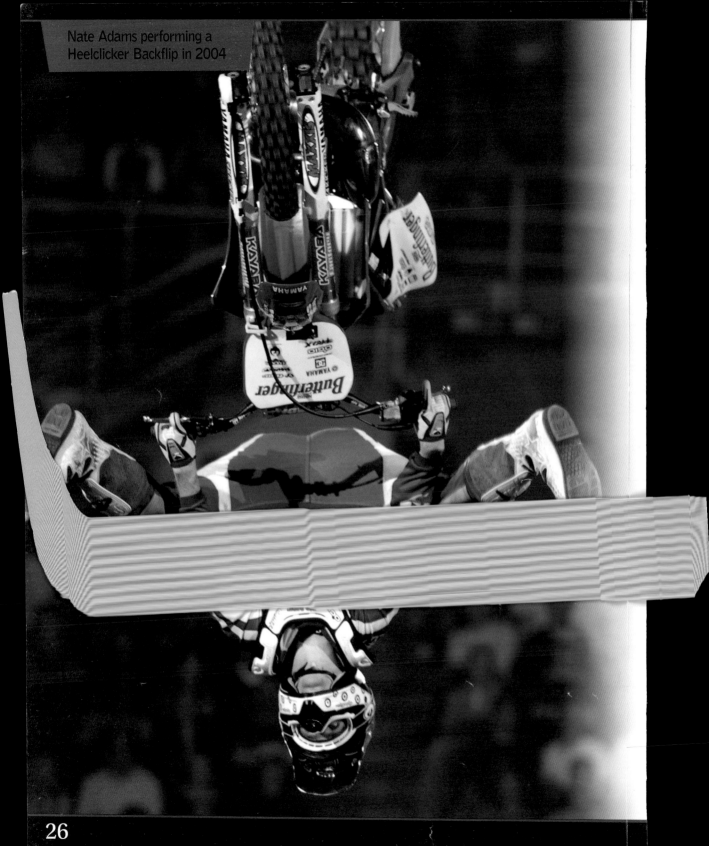

Like many FMX stars, Nate Adams started in motocross racing. He is known for inventing new backflip tricks. New tricks keep fans hooked on FMX.

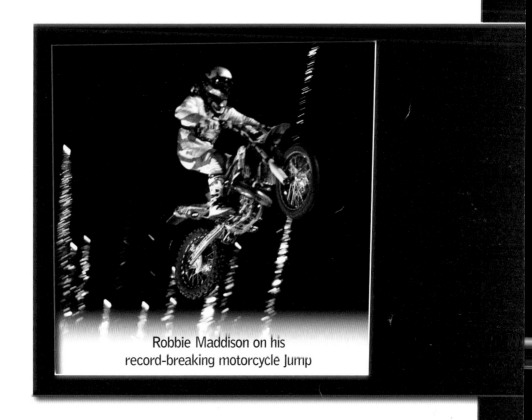

Robbie Maddison on his record-breaking motorcycle jump

Fact: FMX rider Robbie Maddison holds the world record for the longest motorcycle jump. He jumped 351 feet (107 meters) on March 29, 2008.

Freestyle Flipping!

Glossary

armor (AR-muhr)—hard covering that riders wear for protection in crashes

body varial (BAH-dee VAIR-ee-uhl)—a trick in which the rider removes himself from the bike and spins

classic (KLASS-ik)—of good quality and likely to be popular for a long time

combination (kahm-buh-NAY-shun)—a mixture of two or more tricks

motocross (MOH-tuh-cross)—a type of dirt bike race held on outdoor courses

sidesaddle (SIDE-sad-uhl)—when a rider has both feet on one side of the bike

variation (vair-ee-AY-shuhn)—a slight change that makes an old trick into a new trick

Read More

David, Jack. *Moto-x Freestyle.* Torque: Action Sports. Minneapolis: Bellwether Media, 2008.

Levy, Janey. *Freestyle Motocross.* Motocross. New York: PowerKids Press, 2007.

Miller, Connie Colwell. *Moto X Best Trick.* X Games. Mankato, Minn.: Capstone Press, 2008.

Sievert, Terri. *Travis Pastrana: Motocross Legend.* Dirt Bikes. Mankato, Minn.: Capstone Press, 2006.

Internet Sites

FactHound offers a safe, fun way to find Internet sites related to this book. All of the sites on FactHound have been researched by our staff.

Here's all you do:

Visit *www.facthound.com*

FactHound will fetch the best sites for you!

Index